PUFFIN BOOKS

Knightmare

Marty M. Engle and Johnny Ray Barnes, Jr, graduates of the Art Institute of Atlanta, are the creators, writers, designers and illustrators of the *StrangeMatter*® series and the *StrangeMatter*® *World Wide Web* page.

Their interests and expertise range from state-of-the-art 3-D computer graphics and interactive multimedia, to books and scripts (for television and film).

Marty lives in La Jolla, California, with his wife Jana and twin pets, Polly and Oreo.

Johnny Ray lives in Tierrasanta, California, and spends every free moment with his fiancée, Meredith.

More *StrangeMatter*®

Knightmare

Johnny Ray Barnes, Jr

PUFFIN BOOKS

PUFFIN BOOKS

Published by the Penguin Group
Penguin Books Ltd, 27 Wrights Lane, London W8 5TZ, England
Penguin Books USA Inc., 375 Hudson Street, New York, New York 10014, USA
Penguin Books Australia Ltd, Ringwood, Victoria, Australia
Penguin Books Canada Ltd, 10 Alcorn Avenue, Toronto, Ontario, Canada M4V 3B2
Penguin Books (NZ) Ltd, 182–190 Wairau Road, Auckland 10, New Zealand

Penguin Books Ltd, Registered Offices: Harmondsworth, Middlesex, England

First published in the USA by Front Line Art Publishing 1995
Published by Penguin Books Australia 1996
Published in Great Britain in Puffin Books 1996
1 3 5 7 9 10 8 6 4 2

**TO OUR FAMILIES
&
FRIENDS**

(You know who you are.)

"Things are Coming to Life at The Fairfield Museum"

That's what the banner said.

A Tyrannosaurus Rex skeleton threatened to eat the words at the end of the sentence. *Pretty silly*, I thought. The old museum had never been big enough to hold something like that. Maybe in the science building next to it, but never in the history wing.

Then I noticed the scaffolding that framed the arch above the entrance stairs. Someone had taped off one of the four doorways.

"What's going on?" I asked curiously, not expecting anyone to answer.

Someone did.

"Renovation. They're putting in a back door

for you chickens to run out of when you get scared," said Kyle Banner as he passed me, pushing his way to the front of our field trip group. "Don't you know anything, Moonwalker?"

Moonwalker. My new nickname.

Even on a class trip to the museum, I couldn't get any peace. We had just stepped off the bus, and already I felt depressed.

You see, when anyone in the school thinks of the name Mitchell Garrison, they think "coward". Kyle Banner seemed to always want to keep the idea fresh in everyone's minds. If not for that creep, I'd have no problems at all.

"Don't worry about him, Mitchell. He's just trying to get your goat," Keri said to me before walking ahead. She's still my friend, but it's almost like she *has* to be. She's sort of indirectly responsible for what happened, but I have to take most of the blame.

Just a month ago, I led a normal life. I had lots of friends, lots of laughs, and lots of confidence, until that day after school when Kyle Banner decided to harass Keri for not giving him the answers to that morning's English test.

She and I walk home together, so it's natural that I would be there too, when Kyle started giving her trouble.

He'd picked a great location to hassle us, too, just far enough away from the school grounds so no teachers could see. Unfortunately, a lot of kids take that route home, and they stopped to see what was going on. Pretty soon a crowd formed. I felt a million eyes on me, and every one of them expected me to defend myself and Keri's honour. They cheered me on, yelling for me to take a swing, to knock Kyle's block off.

But I didn't. My legs turned to jelly as Kyle's fist loomed in the air, just looking for the perfect spot to pop me. My stomach jerked nervously, and fear took control of my useless body.

I backed away from him.

In those steps, I'd earned my ticket into Fairfield Junior High's Hall of Cowardice, and Kyle dubbed me "Moonwalker", after Michael Jackson's famous dance move. To my horror, the name stuck, and that's what everyone called me.

But the skirmish didn't end there, at least not Kyle's part of it. Trey Porter stepped out from the crowd and did exactly what I should've done. He looked Kyle square in the eyes, and told him if it was a fight he was looking for, he'd found it. The bully sized him up, and looked like

3

he thought Trey could back up his threats. Kyle retreated, but he'd completed his mission.

He destroyed me socially. Even though I backed down, having Trey take care of the mess for me made me look even worse. I thought I'd never live that day down, the most humiliating one of my life. Little did I know how soon that would change.

"Hey, Mitch, are you reliving that day in your head again? You're letting that experience scar your psyche, pal," said Howard. Howard Peel's the only other person besides Keri who will talk to me. He says he's got big plans for how to get me back in good graces with the rest of the class.

"Howard, do you even know what a psyche is?" I asked him. His use of the word smelled of current dictionary perusal.

"Sure. It's the soul or spirit. Do you know what the Deschaul Exhibit is?" Howard threw his question right back at me.

"No. What is it?" I asked him as the class started to move through the three open doors.

"It's the big medieval exhibit old man Deschaul's had hauled to Fairfield from France. It's supposed to be kickin'."

"What's that got to do with the soul or

4

spirit?" I asked.

"Everything. It's got everything to do with repairing *your psyche*. I've got a plan, man."

"Huh?" I asked, but Howard didn't say another word, and we continued through the door.

Our teacher, Mrs. Spearman, hushed the class as we walked into the foyer, which had been expanded on each side. Part of the renovation, I guessed. I found that a little silly, too. Any time they added any major exhibit at all, the museum had to be renovated. It had originally been the old town hall. When Fairfield's new City Hall went up in the late 60s, they converted this building to hold all of the town treasures. At any rate, the more they put in the place, the bigger it got.

"All right, class. I think you all know Mr. Deschaul."

Wow. Mr. René Deschaul himself had offered to show our class around. Everyone knew him as one of the richest men in Fairfield, and also as director of the town's History Museum and Science Centre. I'd only seen him in the paper, though. He looked a lot older in person, with grey hair and big, puffy eyes. He kept tugging at his tight shirt collar that pinched the fat around his neck. When he shuffled his feet, I noticed his stumpy legs and realized that he couldn't be much taller than I am. All of his moving about simply let the class clue in on his nervousness. He wanted to be somewhere else, doing anything else.

"I'll be honest with you, kids. If I had known you were coming today, I would've made Mrs. Handle, our regular guide, reschedule her vacation. But since she's in Bermuda and I'm not, I guess I'll have to run you through some of the new exhibits we've acquired here at the museum."

Hands instantly shot into the air with questions hanging below them. Mr. Deschaul smiled crookedly and took the first three.

"Are there drink machines in the museum now?" Hank Dunk asked in his usual dimwitted manner.

"No," Mr. Deschaul answered.

Then Keri asked, "So there are no dinosaur bones like the banner outside leads you to believe?"

"No, that banner was designed by a free-lance graphic artist who was not on staff and not familiar with what the museum contained. We didn't pay him for the job either, I believe. One more question. Yes, you, young man . . ." He pointed to Howard.

"Yes, sir. Are we going to see the medieval exhibit today?"

Mr. Deschaul's expression grew serious. "Everything in that exhibit's being checked right now and probably won't be set up for another week. But you kids can feel free to come back and see it with your parents. They'll have to pay full price, but you can get in for half of that."

With that questionable welcome, Mr. Deschaul led the entire class to the first room of historical findings.

That's when Howard grabbed the back of my shirt to stop me.

"What is it?" I asked.

"Come on, let's go," he replied, grinning.

"Where?" I asked.

"I think I know where the medieval exhibit is. We're going to sneak in and see it. Let's go." His eyes had that happy dog look in them.

"Mrs. Spearman will murder us," I told him.

"Mrs. Spearman will never know. We'll be in and out in less than a minute."

"I don't know . . ."

"Come on, Mitch," Howard urged. "It'll be cool! And when everyone finds out you saw it, they'll think *you're* cool!"

That sold me.

We backed away from the group, and quickly lost ourselves down one of the long, dark, side halls.

If I had known then what awaited us, I never would have followed.

Our shadows carried themselves across the walls in such a devilish manner, it made sneaking off seem even more criminal than it was.

Howard always did things like this. Some sort of master plan seemed to be brewing in his head all the time, and when one of the better ones struck him, he had to go with it, no matter what the consequences.

"So?" I whispered. "Where is this thing?"

"Here. At the bottom of this ramp. Through that door. That's where they store things. My mom worked here one summer. I know."

Even through the small patch of darkness at the bottom of the incline, I could see that trouble crawled all over that door. Opening it would mean no going back.

"Howard, if we go into that room, man, that's

it. This goes from a slap on the wrist to pure detention. Maybe even suspension."

I saw a look on Howard's face like he'd already been in the room, marvelled at all the great things in there, and now couldn't think of the words to describe its wonders to me. How could I even think about not going in after we'd come this far? That's what he wanted to say.

"Just follow me," Howard replied, and stepped down the ramp to the door.

"No lock?" I couldn't believe they'd just leave the storeroom open.

"I bet Mr. Deschaul was just in here," Howard said. "Let's see what Museum Man's got hidden down here."

Howard pushed the door open. It didn't even creak, but simply swung open into a void so black it looked thick enough to grab. I didn't think about stopping the door, but luckily, Howard did. He jumped after the handle, grasping it and holding the door before it could hit the wall.

I reached in and searched the wall for a light switch. Ouch - something sharp . . . Ewww - something gooey . . . Ah, finally, electricity!

"AAAAGGGGHHHH!"

I screamed.

A person.

In the middle of the room.

Looking right at us.

Howard grabbed me.

"SHUT UP, SHUT UP, shut up! It's just a suit of armour," he said.

"Just a suit of armour? No way. It's amazing." I walked closer to get a better look, catching my reflection in the emerald breastplate.

I'd seen armour in real life before, but this had to be the tallest suit I'd ever run across. In fact, the guy who once wore it could have a starting position on the Chicago Bulls today.

"What do you know about it?" Howard asked. He didn't know I'd had a two-month infatuation with knights in the fourth grade. I'd read all about them and drawn them every day. I'd even made my own suit of armour out of cardboard boxes. It had actually held up for a week or so, until it got rained on.

"Well, this wasn't made for some flat foot infantry man, that's for sure. This armour's royal. Check out the colour. How'd they do that? And I'm surprised with this much metal to work with, the owner didn't want it detailed with cool designs or the family crest." Information seemed to spill out of me. I hadn't gone on about something like this for a long time. That ominous metal suit someone may have died in centuries ago gave me something to get excited about.

"Well, expert, choose your weapon!" With some difficulty, Howard lifted a mace into the air and took several wide steps toward me, trying to keep the weapon steady as he approached.

"Put the mace down. You'll kill yourself," I said.

He let it drop a little too hard to the floor, then looked around for something else to threaten me with.

He picked up a crossbow, and pointed it at the armour.

"Howard, don't!" I warned as loudly as I could.

"Do you ever read that comic, *Spearhead, the Crime Hunter*? He uses one of these things. In fact, he laid out Arsenal, the one-man weapon, with a crossbow. It was the only thing that would pierce the bad guy's armour."

"Just put it down," I begged.

"What's that thing around its neck?" Howard asked.

A round, silver disk, about a quarter of an inch thick, hung by a leather strap from the base of the armour's helmet.

"I think it's a die for sealing," I answered, and then explained. "Some knights and noblemen couldn't read or write, so instead of signing documents, they'd just add a wax seal pressed from their own metal die. That's what this is, I think. His own personal seal-maker."

Howard wanted to continue his questions when we heard something from the far side of the room.

The noise came from another door.

Its handle turned to open.

3

Howard dove under a nearby table.

The lights! Whoever it was would notice the lights!

I moved over to the wall and flipped off the switch, then sank quickly to the floor just as daylight flooded the room.

The overhead lights revealed a lot more than the sun did. From the open doorway, my spot at the far end of the room couldn't be seen very well. The shadows hid me. Still, that rat Howard had the best hiding place. I'd brain him good if we got out of here without getting caught.

Two figures stepped inside the room.

As soon as he spoke, I instantly recognized the first man's voice.

"How secure are things?" the deep, low voice asked.

Ivan.

Fairfield's Chief-of-Security.

Whenever someone wanted something looked over, they called on Ivan Brewer.

Every kid in town knew him. He kept you away from things. But how hard could that be for a guy who looked like one of those nightmarish bald, bearded, wrestler types, with a badge? The badge meant security, not police, which meant that if he caught you, he didn't have to take you to jail. He could do whatever he wanted. I'd heard horrible stories about kids who Ivan supposedly caught in the past, who had never been heard from again. Now the kids at school would talk about how Mitchell Garrison just disappeared!

"We wheeled everything down here last night," said the other man, obviously a museum worker. "Mr. Deschaul wanted an inventory of everything this morning, but he had to take over that field trip tour."

"You'd think he would have been anxious enough to check everything last night," said Ivan. His voice never changed tone at all. "This is his ancestry, after all. His family heritage. You'd think he'd show more interest."

"Oh, he's interested, all right. He told me he was giving those kids the quick, thirty-minute tour, and then he'd grab his catalogue and be right down," said the other man.

"Well, if this stuff's going to stay down here another night, this door's going to need another lock. I bet that one over there does, too."

I heard the footsteps coming my way. My body tensed and I tried to crawl away on my toes and finger tips, but Ivan came too fast. Dread's heavy blanket draped over my head, and under its weight I lowered my face to the floor and felt the cold concrete against my cheek. I wondered if my shirt would stretch or just rip under the strain of Ivan yanking me up by the collar and lifting me into the air to peer into his black eyes. I didn't want it to end like this . . .

And then . . .

"Yeah, that one's got the same crummy lock, Mr. Brewer," the other guy said.

Ivan stopped and turned around. "Okay, then. Let's go over to Zimmerman's for some special locks. I know just the kind we need."

A few seconds after the door closed behind them, I felt the hand on my shoulder.

I practically jumped across the room.

Howard.

He snickered quietly, but uncontrollably.

"You couldn't think that was funny," I snapped. "That was Ivan, man! He almost had me!"

"S-sorry, I can't help it. Some things are just so terrifying they make me laugh." Howard continued to chuckle.

"Strange. It didn't have that effect on me. Let's go back. You heard the other guy. Deschaul's giving them a short tour," I said.

"Yeah, I heard him. And it gave me an idea for a plan. A perfect plan for your revenge against Kyle Banner." Howard motioned me over to the suit of armour.

"What are you talking about?" I asked.

"Ivan said that all this stuff was Deschaul's

family heirlooms. That includes this armour, and this die-seal around its neck." Howard's eyes got wider as he explained his master plan in more detail.

"So what?" I asked, trying to force his point so we could get out of there.

"So you take this die, and put a wax seal on a few anonymous notes and send them to Mr. Deschaul. That will really torque him off after a while because he doesn't know who has it, but obviously someone does. Then, in a couple of weeks, you sneak the die into Kyle Banner's locker, and we tip off Mr. Deschaul that the bully's got his heirloom. It'd be awesome!"

Howard had seriously fallen off his rocker.

"Are you leaking brain from the head? That's stealing. There's no way," I told him.

"What? What do you mean, stealing? Oh, you mean like how Kyle stole all of your dignity on the way home from school that day? I'd say it's a small price to pay to get back at that bully in spades. Besides, Mr. Deschaul gets the die back." Howard continued to push his scheme on me as I kept remembering Banner's face mocking me and making me look stupid.

With every passing second, I became more

and more convinced.

Finally Howard said, "Look, Mitch, if you want to beat the bad guy, you've got to think like a bad guy."

At the time, it sounded reasonable enough. Besides, he'd pumped me so full of anger for Kyle in the last few seconds that I'd have driven a bulldozer over the bully's grandmother's house.

In a head-spinning decision, I removed the die from around the knight's neck.

"Okay," I said. "Let's go."

Regret has to be the worst feeling in the world. Well, there's guilt, too, but that usually comes with regret like some kind of soul-judging combo meal; regret, guilt, and just a side serving of paranoia.

What had I been thinking?

Revenge.

Howard had talked me into making the worst mistake of my life. The very fact that everything had gone just as he'd planned made me even more certain that somehow, in some way, a reckoning awaited me.

We reunited with our group, undetected. I waited through the rest of the day in school with the seal-maker in my pocket. When I got home, I went directly to my room and hid the die under my bed. Howard's plan called for us to send our first sealed note to Mr. Deschaul the next day.

That night I couldn't sleep.

At least, not at first.

The stress of the day had taxed my nerves to their limit, but finally my eyelids closed and my body shut down . . .

Leaving my mind free to dream . . .

Max Chandler woke me up. I was confused for a few seconds, but then I realized I was in English class, where I'd fallen asleep, and Mrs. Spearman had just noticed my snoring. I guess the whole thing had been a dream!

That made sense. How could I ever steal anything? I've always been a good kid. Nothing could ever push me to that, could it? I looked over at Howard sitting near the front of the class. Mrs. Spearman had moved him there earlier in the year for causing trouble in the back.

I'll never listen to Howard again, I thought. He'll only get me into trouble.

"Class, we have a special visitor today." Mrs. Spearman called us to order. "He's going to try to teach us all something about consequences. Do any of you know what consequences are?"

Keri's hand quickly shot up in the air. "They are the after-effects of a certain action," she answered. Keri is one of the biggest brains in our class.

"That's right, Keri," said my teacher. "And to tell you more about them, I'd like to introduce you to the Count Deschaul."

In the next instant, I knew things couldn't be real.

Metal scraping across the floor. It sounded like footsteps! My brain pulsed with messages of *No, it can't be* and *This is not happening*, but my heart didn't listen. It pounded so hard I could taste it at the top of my throat.

Mr. Deschaul's family legacy, the emerald suit of armour, walked through our classroom door.

My lower jaw dropped at the sight of the slow-moving metallic soldier as it strode to the front of the classroom and turned to face us. A green, glowing mist seeped from its visor, and I couldn't even tell if the suit held anyone inside.

Beads of sweat dotted my forehead as I waited for it to make its move.

It simply stood there, motionless.

I had to get out of there! I had to move! It wanted me to pay for what I'd done! I knew it!

I trembled so hard I couldn't stay in my seat, so I didn't even bother trying. Sliding out of my desk, I felt my legs go dead. When I fell to the floor, my hands took over, helping me crawl backwards despite the lack of cooperation from my feet.

A hint of red light was building behind the green fog that leaked from the knight's face, and soon it bathed the entire room with a coat of vermillion.

"**Mitchell Garrison**," a slithering, amplified voice drummed in my head. "**Please stand up.**"

My judgement was at hand.

How and why I got up, I do not know. But I did. The only feeling I had in my entire body came from the cursed hairs that kept standing up on the back of my neck. I hunched my shoulders against them, but they wouldn't stop. I let it go, choosing to fidget rather than making an awkward scratch.

The room had become so dry and hot that a tall glass of water became the only thought on my mind, until the knight spoke again.

"**What are the consequences for the things you have done?**" it asked.

I tried to swallow. It went down like a rock. I knew that answer already.

"D-death?" I answered.

The knight replied by laughing at me. It echoed through my head, shaking the room and almost stopping my heart.

Then he ceased.

"**Very often**," he said. "**Others pay for your actions!**"

He held out his hand, and to my surprise, Keri stood up. She slowly made her way up to the front of the class to stand beside the emerald knight.

"Keri? What are you doing?" I asked.

Her eyes widened and she opened her mouth to scream to me, but the knight's metal glove covered it. Then the light in his visor began to flicker, like it had a bad connection, then went out altogether.

When the light disappeared, so did the knight and Keri.

"KERI!" I yelled, and then scoured the eyes of my classmates. They had to get out of their seats! They had to help me find Keri!

That's when I noticed the steam.

It came from their heads, their eyes, their mouths, from every part of them. An undertone of moans came from only a few of them at first, but soon the whole room filled with the howling sounds of my school friends.

The skin on their faces began to move, sliding down their cheeks and dripping onto their desks.

They all began to melt.

I couldn't get the scream out before I heard someone calling my name from the classroom door.

"**Over here, my friend! Over here!**" said the man. Another knight, but this one wasn't wearing a helmet. He looked sincere, like he wanted to help me, and at this point I was ready to trust anyone who offered.

I caught a quick glance of Howard bubbling over his English homework and spilling to the floor. Mrs. Spearman had oozed all over our book reports, setting the notebooks aflame.

I jetted out into the hallway, and a rush of air slammed the door behind me, bringing an end to the ghastly shrieking that still echoed in my ears.

The unmasked knight approached me. That's when I noticed the hole where his heart should have been. I could see right through it to the set of lockers behind him.

"**Go after Deschaul**," he said. "**Save your friend**."

"How do I know you're my friend?" I asked him.

"**Because you have my missing piece**,"

he replied, and then simply faded away.

I had no idea what he meant.

A thick, yellow fog began to fill the halls, and I heard sounds coming from the east end, toward the school's entrance.

I started in that direction, realizing that this had to be a dream. The unforgivable crime I'd committed that day had manifested into possibly the worst nightmare I'd ever had in my life, and the only way to wake up would be to see this thing through to the end.

Something big moved in the fog.

I listened closely.

Could I really be hearing this?

Snorting?

That's when an unnaturally large shadow fell over me, and the snorting became a snarl.

A giant. That's what it had to be. It wore a helmet that scratched the hallway ceiling, and one of its legs made up two of me. It stepped out of the fog to grab me. The light from the windows started disappearing so quickly from the mist, I could barely make out enough of my attacker to avoid it. I managed to get away from it, pressing myself against the wall, and feeling along it with my hands as I ran.

With those huge legs, it must've had gargantuan feet. I became deathly afraid of it stepping on me. I couldn't see it any more to get out of the way.

Then I realized how awful the thing smelled. It reeked of rotted food and dirty animals. If I got a strong sniff of that smell, I'd know . . .

My fingers ran across an anomaly in the wall.

A small door? A fire extinguisher. A weapon.

I pulled it from its case quickly. That's when the smell of bursting trash bags and overflowing garbage disposals cleared my sinuses.

Behind me. *It's right behind me.*

As I turned, I saw the giant moving through the mist, revealing its misshapen face.

My fog giant had the face of a pig, coupled with two stained tusks jutting from the sides of a mouth that dripped with spit. From its chin hung a long, grey beard that ran mid-way to its round gut, where something leaked from its bellybutton down to the bugs that crawled through its fur loincloth. Its boots glistened from something it had recently squashed, and it dragged its huge, wooden club through that same gelatinous muck on the floor . . .

Until it saw me.

Then it raised the club into the air, ready to bring it down on my head. I knew it was over, so I just threw the extinguisher as hard as I could and screamed.

I heard a crash.

I'd broken a window! I'd missed the beast completely!

Then an inhuman howl, much like the one

I'd heard from my classmates before, erupted from the monster's lungs as the light from outside struck its head. It ruptured and burst, and a shower of yellow jelly, with bits of tusks in it, rained on the floor. The creature collapsed, its shoulders striking the wall beside me, putting a hole there the size of . . .

a wild boar.

A WILD BOAR? That's what stepped through the wall, and over the monster I'd just defeated.

It had to be as big as a small car. Honda size. It, too, had tusks, but unlike the monster before, it was all animal, and looked ten times more vicious. Flies circled and crawled over its head as it sniffed at the jelly on the floor. It licked up a good gallon of the stuff before it noticed me backing away and turning the corner.

I pictured in my mind what it looked like when it snarled the way it did. That image was like jet fuel for me. Every part of my brain focused on one job.

Run.

My legs cooperated. As I heard the frothing beast round the corner, I was already more than halfway down the hall.

Its hooves dug into the floor as it shot after me, that much I could hear. But mostly I felt its huffs, its shrieks, and its growls.

The mist still filled the halls. It seemed to grow thicker as I ran, and whiffs of it burnt my nose. Tears welled up and poured from my eyes. I could hardly see!

Where was I?

I'd lost my sense of direction!

The savage, wild boar closed in on me, ready to gnaw me to the bone, and I couldn't see to get away!

I closed my eyes tightly, trying to clear my vision.

When I opened my eyes, I saw someone else running directly toward me!

As I got closer, I realized . . .

It was me! It was my reflection!

I tried to stop, but in doing so I tripped, hit the ground, and rolled to a stop right next to the school's trophy case in the lobby.

I tried to get to my feet in time, but . . .

The boar ran head first into the glass front of the case.

The glass shattered and fell around me, but I rolled away, intending to put as much distance between myself and the beast as possible.

No hurry. The boar's body crumpled and lowered to the floor, its head still stuck in the glass. It didn't move.

Getting up, I shook the remaining shards of glass from my clothes, then felt air blow in behind me and saw light cut through the swirling fog layer.

"*Mitchell Garrison*," said an unfamiliar voice. "*Come out.*"

Whoever spoke to me sounded calm, almost soothing. To hear someone speak to me like that at this point in my nightmare could be considered a port in a storm.

This has to be close to the end, I thought. It made sense. Walking out of the dark building and into the sunlight would symbolise waking up. I had to be close to finding Keri and the evil knight.

The warm glow on my face only hinted at what majesty followed. As the fog curled and disappeared around me, I stepped forth onto the base of something grand.

A wide, stone stairway leading to the entrance of a marvellous castle that floated above the school, on top of low lying clouds.

A dream world.

I peered up at the top of the stairs and saw the knight settled on a throne, with Keri seated on the stair next to him. She looked empty, with no hope left in her at all.

I stepped closer, and once again heard the calming voice.

"*You have come to do battle with Count Deschaul. You*

must first pass this gate," it said.

The last remnants of haze lifted and my eyes met the face of a new horror.

It perched itself on a column next to a tall, iron gate that blocked the stairway. The creature looked deceptively like a giant eagle at first, but when it lowered its head to me, I noticed paws where its clawed feet should've been. It had a lion's body. Wheels started spinning in my head. I jerked open mental filing cabinets and pillaged through them. I'd read about these things. This thing had a name . . .

"To pass this gate," it said, *"you must guess my name. You have three guesses."*

Oh, great. *Think, Mitchell, think of the name . . .*

"And if you do not guess correctly, I will chew off your head," it finished saying.

Added pressure. I rummaged through old memories, seeking those two months where I had been obsessed with medieval history and lore. Those monsters, with the head and wings of an eagle and the body of a lion, were called . . .

"Griffin! You're a griffin!" I announced, loud and proud.

"A griffin is what I am, but it is not my name.

I don't call you boy, do I? Two more guesses."

AAGGGHHH. A proper name? This monster wants me to guess its proper name? I searched my mind desperately for a clue, anything that would give me the beast's handle. Bob, Stanley, Ross, Jimmy Dean? What? What could it be?

Wait! Yes! It was so obvious!

"Griffin!" I said to him, "Your name's Griffin!"

"Griffin . . . the griffin? J'm afraid not. J would not advise guessing Griffin again. The only outcome will be your head entering my mouth, which, J'm sorry to say young man, is likely to happen anyway. Come now, one more guess."

I had no choice. My hand slowly made its way to my neck and caressed it, thinking about what could be just seconds away from happening. I focused on the ground, thinking, searching, fighting back the fear of being chewed.

A piece of paper wrapped itself around my ankle. I bent down and picked it up. Flipping it over, I saw a bunch of black shapes.

Just a jumble of images with no meaning at all.

"*What? What is that?*" asked the griffin.

I gulped and turned the paper towards him, showing him the design on the other side. The beast studied it, hardly moving except for the periodic blinking of its eyes.

"*You may enter,*" it said.

The gates creaked open and I stepped back to let them swing by.

The words had the hardest time making their way through to my brain. I can enter? How? What did the griffin see in that design that I didn't? That's when I recalled a documentary on dreams I'd watched one time. Some specialists say you can't read the written word in your dreams. The writing is often seen as garbled lines, simple designs or drawings. The griffin's name! That's what was on that piece of paper in the form of simple little shapes!

I don't know who drew it or how it got to me, but the contents on that sheet of paper saved my skin. I didn't have time to worry about it. I figured I'd sort it out later.

And now, to save Keri.

As I climbed the stairs, the suit of armour got to its feet. Keri moved away from it, sliding over a few feet, but total, petrifying fear kept her from running.

Once again, the light cast from his visor washed over everything in sight. The whole scene looked as if I was seeing it through a red filter. My only comforting thought, *this nightmare would be ending soon.*

"**So the boy has come to have judgement passed on him for his criminal deeds. Are you willing to pay the price?**" asked the knight.

The sight of this metal man lowering himself down the stairs in my direction had to be the most intimidating image so far. Unlike the monster in the hall, or the boar, I knew I'd have to face him. And unlike the griffin, he'd give me no chances. If I ever wanted to tell myself I wasn't a coward, even in my dreams, I'd have to answer him now.

"I just want Keri back," I answered.

"**So.**" He stopped his descent. "**Come get her. And bring this.**" He pulled a sword out of thin air and tossed it down the stairs to me. Then he conjured up his own, and returned to the top of the stairs to await my confrontation.

So this is how it ends, I thought, referring to the dream. It'd really be a nightmare to have things happen this way in the real world.

The sword didn't budge on my first attempt to pick it up. Using both hands, I managed to pull it up, and once my entire back was into it, I lifted the weapon in the air. The thing weighed a ton.

How could I fight him if I couldn't even hold my sword up?

I didn't take the extra time to stop and worry about it. I just wanted this whole adventure over with. Besides, I'd already beaten the first three monsters. I was on a roll! How could I possibly lose the final showdown?

All noise seemed to die out as I reached the top of the stairs. Only Keri's whimpers could be heard before the knight lifted his sword, and brought it down across mine.

The force of the blow instantly knocked the weapon from my hands.

Somewhere from the back of my mind the word "chivalry" sprang; a knight's moral code, a courteous and civil way to deal with one's enemies. In the spirit of this ideal, I hoped I'd be given the chance to pick up my sword again.

But the knight didn't have a chivalrous bone in his body.

He continued to swing at me. I dodged his blade again and again, trying to find the one thing that would beat him, but I had no idea what that could be.

"Keri, help!" I cried. She just sat there like a little baby, a bump on a log. "Help me find something to beat this guy!"

The knight swung at my legs and I jumped over the blade, making my way to Keri. I grabbed her and shook her fiercely, trying to rattle her brain to life.

"KERI, HELP! KERI, CAN YOU HEAR ME? HELP!"

That's when I felt the steel glove seize the back of my shirt and hoist me into the air.

"**We are almost done here**," the knight thundered, and threw me onto the throne chair.

I landed so hard that the air left my lungs. My enemy moved in front of me, not allowing me any chance for escape.

"**When you are out there, in the real world, be sure not to cross my path. Dreams can become reality. Do not forget that.**" the knight warned, then lifted his sword.

Behind him, I saw the vision of the good knight I'd encountered before, the one that led me on the quest to begin with.

"Help," I begged.

"**You already have all the help I can give you**," said the good knight.

I looked up, just in time to see the sword coming down and hear the knight yelling out, "**I AM RETURNING!**"

And then everything went black . . .

9

I woke up shaking, trying to scream through a dry throat. Only a wheezing sigh passed my lips. My eyes desperately searched for a light, any light, so I would know it had all been a dream, and I still resided in the land of the living. Gripping my chest with an open hand, I breathed in deeply at least a dozen times, focusing on the blowing drapes at my open window.

Mom never liked me leaving the window open, not even a crack, but I'm glad I did that night. The slight breeze and beaming moonlight told me nothing had changed.

Nothing had changed. That meant . . .

I grabbed frantically under my mattress to check. When my fingers wrapped around the warm steel of the seal-making die, a bubbling dread began to dissolve the walls of my stomach.

40

As long as the seal maker stayed in my possession, I knew I'd always be looking over my shoulder.

It had to be returned.

10

Walking into Mrs. Spearman's English class the next day gave me quite a morbid feeling. I would have called it grief, but the fact that no one talked to me except to call me "Moonwalker" reminded me that my class hadn't changed either. I actually trembled a little when I sat at my desk, and found myself gripping the desktop tightly just to calm myself down.

"You're not as sneaky as you thought," Keri whispered in my ear as she passed me on the way to her desk.

She knew? How did she know? Did everybody know?

Oh, no. My mind agonized over all the possible outcomes. Howard and I are going to jail.

I watched Howard stroll into the room and take his seat. He glanced back at me, winked, and gave me the thumbs up.

What a moron, I thought. *Doesn't he realize everyone knows?*

Then Mrs. Spearman came in. Her stone-serious face confirmed my fear. Howard and I were doomed.

My nails dug into the desktop even further, and I tried desperately to stop shaking as Mrs. Spearman spoke.

"I don't know how often any of you read the papers, but it seems they had some trouble at the museum yesterday and it made the front page," she announced. "Someone has stolen a valuable artefact."

Sherlock Holmes would've busted a gut laughing at the simplicity of solving this case. With one glance over the classroom, any second-rate sleuth with even a minor degree in investigation could have told you who took that artefact. That would be the kid in the second row, third from the back. The pale, trembling one who looks as if he's about to get sick.

Me, Mrs. Spearman. Just tell everyone it was me and let's get it over with. I felt myself about to crack. Howard looked back at me, saw my nervous state, and looked a little uneasy himself.

Mrs. Spearman continued. "Mr. Deschaul wanted to speak with you about this incident, so he's come here today. Class, say hello again to Mr. Deschaul."

The utter shock of seeing our guest walk into the classroom the day after my vivid nightmare stopped my shakes. An unnerving fascination pushed my guilt aside for the moment. Not a coincidence, I thought. It's too much like the dream.

"Hello again, kids," Mr. Deschaul said. "As Mrs. Spearman has told you, we've had a burglary at the museum. A rare, silver seal-die, used for pressing wax seals to documents, was taken from our storeroom yesterday. It hung from the neck of a suit of armour belonging to my great ancestor, the Count Deschaul of France."

Count Deschaul. The knight from my dream. That was *his* name.

"What makes this matter even more pressing," Mr. Deschaul continued, "are the stories I've heard from curators of the French museum I requested the exhibit from. They seem to believe that if the armour and the die were ever separated, ill winds and bad spirits would blow through the land of its acquisition."

I believed that. I totally believed that.

"I do not believe in curses of any kind," Deschaul summed up. "I simply want what is mine and that of the history museum returned, and if we are saving Fairfield some bad fortune by doing so, then we're also performing a community service. To make things go quicker, I've offered a five thousand dollar reward for any information leading to its return. So if you have any information at all, please see me in your principal's office after class."

I felt my heart pounding again as Mr. Deschaul left the room. If someone knew what Howard and I had done, they'd surely go tell Deschaul for five thousand dollars. I watched the class closely, ready for any accusing looks from my peers. I only got one.

From Keri.

She knew. As the rest of the class tried to solve the mystery amongst themselves, I felt a huge boulder where my stomach used to be.

Mrs. Spearman gave us the rest of the class time to do book report research in the library if we wished.

The whole library smelled of insecticide from a recent de-bugging, so most of the class got in there, then got right back out. But Howard and

I stayed, and soon Keri joined us at our own private table.

"What do you know?" Howard asked her. I'd told him what she whispered to me.

"I know you did it. I don't know which one of you actually has it, but I know you disappeared while we were being shown around, and reappeared right before we left."

"Does anybody else know?" I asked.

"Not that I can tell. Most everybody kept running from exhibit to exhibit, talking uncontrollably and getting called down by Mrs. Spearman," she said.

Howard leaned in. "How did you know we were missing?"

"I keep tabs on you guys," she said, and then looked at me. "So what are you going to do? Tip off Mr. Deschaul to where it is, and collect five thousand dollars?"

Howard's eyes lit up. "That is the plan, yes."

"That's not our plan," I countered.

"That's our new plan," Howard snapped back.

"What *was* your plan?" Keri asked.

"We were going to pin the whole thing on Kyle Banner," I said. She looked at me with a full understanding of why I'd do that, but I could still see a little disappointment in her eyes. "But we're not going to do that now," I told her.

"Yeah, we're going to be rich, instead," said Howard.

"No, we're not going to be rich, either. I've got a new plan, and it's much tougher than either one of those," I announced.

"So my plans are easy. So what? That's what makes them good plans, Mitch. Tell me your tough plan, and I'll tell you if it's any good," Howard raved.

I leaned in, letting Howard and Keri know I meant business. "My plan is . . . we sneak back into the museum, and return the die."

They both stared at me.

"That's not a good plan, Mitch," Howard said.

"Well, good plan or bad plan, it's my plan and I'm doing it," I told them.

"Why? Why do you want to sneak it back in there? You'll get caught, for sure." Keri expressed her concern by grabbing my hand and squeezing. She didn't want me getting into trouble.

I knew my reasoning for returning the die was just as questionable as our intentions were for taking it in the first place. But if they really wanted to know why I wanted to go back to the museum, I'd tell them.

"Those things Mr. Deschaul talked about? You know, the seal maker and the curse; I think he's more right than he knows," I explained. "I had a nightmare last night, and if I don't return the artefact to the museum, I'm afraid that bad dream's going to come true."

Recollections of the dream came to me instantly. I had no problem remembering every horror I'd encountered, or every word I'd spoken along the way. Howard became disinterested after his own death in the dream, but Keri hung on each syllable up until the end. The retelling of that final image, of the sword striking me down, had me shaking all over again.

"So, let me get this straight," said Howard. "You want to get into four lifetimes of trouble all at once because you were spooked by a bad dream?"

"It's more than that." I hadn't wanted to mention the good knight's appearance. It seemed doing it now might be just too crazy. "I have this feeling. I just know that if I don't return that die, the knight's going to come after me. And I'm going to wake up in my bed one night, and see that sword come down again. Only then, it's going to be for keeps."

11

That night, I found myself on the receiving end of a mind-numbing interrogation. Leave it to Howard to thoroughly question any plan that didn't come from his own head.

"So you think we're going to waltz back into the museum, and just put the seal-maker back around the suit of armour's neck?" he asked.

"Somehow we've got to. The knight's going to come after me if we don't give it back to him," I replied.

"Mitchell, please," Howard begged. "Just listen to me for one second. I've been going along with you all day, but now you've got to listen to me. I know this dream's got you spooked. I know you wished you'd never picked up that seal, but don't you think sneaking out of the house is going just a little bit too far?"

We had walked maybe a mile since we left Howard's house. I'd left my window open that night, climbed out into the tree beside my house, and made my way over to Howard's. He met me in his bushes, according to the plan that I put together on the way home from school.

It's funny that when breaking a rule is Howard's idea, it's fun for him. When it's mine, it's a grave error. But unlike Howard, breaking rules never came naturally to me, and the ends always had to justify the means. They rarely did, so I rarely broke the rules.

"All I'm saying, Mitch, is that we need to think about this logically," pleaded Howard. "Why can't we just send this thing to Deschaul through the mail? Or just leave it on some teacher's desk with an anonymous note?"

"Howard, you didn't have the dream. If you did, you'd want the seal-maker back where it belongs as bad as I do," I argued.

"I do, I do," said my jittery friend. "But I don't see any sense in getting in any trouble over it. No one has to know you and I are returning it. That's all I'm saying. Why don't we just leave it on the front steps?"

Maybe Howard was right. Maybe I'd gotten

a little too crazy. I'd just never been that scared before. I wanted so badly to correct my mistake that I didn't want to leave it up to anyone else to do, be it the mail service, a teacher, or otherwise.

"So what do you want to do?" Howard asked.

"Well, I want to do the right thing," I said. "But you're right. There are ways of doing the right thing without getting thrown in the slammer. We'll leave it on the steps."

Howard sighed with relief for what seemed a full minute, and then said, "Cool. I just wish you'd made that decision before we snuck out of the house. But hey, we're out anyway, so let's get this over with."

The pressure of cutting a dreaded task in half made us a lot less tense. Getting punished for sneaking out of the house would be secondary to being found with this artefact in our possession.

It took about thirty minutes to get to the museum. We took the route over Sawyer's Bridge, then down Cameron Court, where the street lights never work, and then through a field and up behind the museum.

Everything seemed okay.

With exhibits being stolen right from under their noses, I expected to see the whole place lit up to deter repeat offenders.

But they'd left everything dark.

Howard and I stood at the edge of the small, wooded brush we had to come through to reach the museum. He motioned for us to circle around, just to check out the front, but still staying close to the trees in case we had to make a break for it.

I still couldn't get over the darkness. Did the dead street lights from Cameron carry over to the museum's frontage street as well? It made me nervous.

"I don't like it," Howard whispered. "Everything's too still. And it's way too dark."

"What do you think we should do?" I asked him.

He kept looking at the museum, trying to get some kind of reading from it. Then he said, "Throw it."

"What? I'm not going to throw it! This thing's an antique! It's more than an antique, it's irreplaceable! I didn't bring it this far just to destroy it!" I quietly argued.

"Then go up there and put it on the stairs, or wherever you feel it will be safe," Howard said. "I swear, Mitchell, I don't think I'm ever going to let you plan anything again. You're just no good at it."

"I've got an idea," I said. "After this, let's just forget all the plans, okay? Good plans, bad plans, tough plans, house plans, or any plans. I think that if we were any good at making them, we wouldn't have to make so many."

With that, I stepped out from the trees, and dropped down close to the ground. I'd seen enough war movies to know that if you just walk up to a suspicious building, you usually get your head shot off. Since I didn't know what awaited me there, I didn't want to take any chances.

Besides, I only had to make it to the steps.

Then the clouds moved away from the moon, and its light showed me something I hadn't seen before.

A tiny reflection.

Something just above the doorway at the front entrance.

Video cameras. Pointed directly at the stairs, so every patron could be studied, every suspect could be logged, and every criminal could be caught on tape.

Very clever, but this wouldn't be a problem for me. I changed my direction, and moved over into the shrubbery beside the stairs. I'd just place the seal-maker on the concrete banister that ran up the stairs. The camera would never see me.

I made my way to the banister. As I stretched up to reach the top of it, I heard the front doors to the museum open.

I dropped down, sucking in every bit of air I could, and remained motionless.

Heavy footsteps carried their way down the stairs, then into the grass, crushing the blades loudly as they strode.

And then it turned the corner.

From there, even through the black veil of night, the moonlight helped reveal the stalking terror.

Ivan.

12

My entire body stiffened as the merciless dog-soldier stalked past, just a few feet in front of me.

He didn't see me, but it wouldn't be long before he noticed.

He wore night-vision goggles. I'd seen a couple of Sasquatch hunters talking about them on television. The goggles gave a green field of vision to whoever used them, but they could see perfectly in the dark. It must have been Ivan who shut off all of the lights around.

But what concerned me the most had to be what he carried. Even in the bad light I could tell it was a gun. I didn't know whether it shot bullets, grenades, or knock-out darts, and I prayed I wouldn't have to find out.

His head moved from side to side, almost

like a robot, as he scanned the area, looking for the slightest movement.

Then he caught something, and started walking straight for the edge of the trees.

HOWARD.

He'd seen Howard moving in the brush. That crazy man was going to shoot my best friend!

A hand grabbed my shoulder.

I jerked so hard I lost my balance. My feet slid out from under me and my rear end hit the ground.

The noise alerted Ivan. He turned around and started moving slowly over toward my position. I tried to stay aware of him but,

I couldn't believe what I saw . . .

The good knight. The one from my dream. A faint blue aura surrounded him, and his eyes stared directly into mine. He knelt on one knee right beside me, with his hand on my shoulder, bracing me for what he had to say to me. An electrical wave coursed through my body, goading me to jump as his mouth moved to speak.

"You, and only you, can return the seal to its rightful place, set upon the breast-plate of Count Deschaul. He wishes to

return to this earth. You, Mitchell, have lived my tragic end through your dream, thereby claiming all rights as keeper of my good soul. Use it to correct your mistake, otherwise all is lost . . ."

He vanished into vapour, leaving my senses to focus on the mangler that approached me, and I realized there wouldn't even be a chance to run away.

"NOW'S OUR CHANCE! RUN!" Howard shouted.

Ivan heard him loud and clear, and moved his head to catch sight of Howard running in the dark. I guess the glasses didn't work very well, because in the next instant he threw them to the ground and produced a wide angle flashlight. A wire led from it to what must have been a battery attached to the security man's pocket. Ivan scanned the trees with the huge light, saw something move, then stormed into the brush after what must have been Howard.

The entire last few seconds had turned my body into rubber. I clasped the seal that lay in my pocket, wanting to slap it on the banister and be gone.

But after what I'd just seen . . .

After what I'd just heard . . .

I couldn't make myself do it.

Getting to my feet, I circled back around the museum, jumping into the brush at the point we came in from, crashing through the branches and small trees that made up the tiny patch of woods.

My heart pumped so hard it made my head pound. Visions of that knight's face filled my mind. A ghost. It looked like a ghost.

When I came out at the other end, I jumped to the bottom of a tiny hill and landed in a ditch bordering the dark cul-de-sac called Cameron Court.

I listened for any sound whatsoever.

Any clue of Howard . . . or Ivan.

Nothing.

I kept looking around, half expecting to see the spectral knight pop up somewhere.

I saw a ghost, I kept telling myself.

I stood up, and stepped out onto the road.

Something crashed into the mound of leaves at the bottom of the ditch.

I started to run, but . . .

"Mitch! Wait!" Howard called quietly.

"I can't believe you!" I said. "What were you thinking, man?"

"I was thinking about saving your hide, Ninja boy. Godzilla, King of the Monsters, could've snuck up on that place better than you!" he replied.

"Where's Ivan?" I asked, scanning the woods for the crazed security man.

Howard chuckled a little. "I doubled back on the goon. He's hauling it up to Main Street. When Sheriff Drake sees that oompa parading around the streets with a firearm, he'll throw him in the pen for a week. Did you leave the seal?"

"Uh, no. I didn't. We've got to think of something else," I said.

"Something else? What do you mean something else?" Howard began to rave.

"I'll explain on the way home," I said, and led the way down the dark pavement of Cameron Court.

When you really want to get home, it always seems to take you longer than usual to get there. As we walked the moonlit street and I fended off Howard's questioning of my actions, it seemed to me that the street would never end. I wanted to get home, sneak in undetected, and creep down to the kitchen for an after-midnight snack. Maybe some leftover turkey, or maybe a big piece of cake to settle my nerves. I could almost smell it.

I could definitely smell something.

A familiar smell, but I couldn't place from where . . .

It smelled like . . . rotted food and dirty animals, with a hint of bursting trash bags and overflowing garbage disposals.

My blood turned to ice.

13

"Do you smell something?" asked Howard.

The gurgling snort behind us put an end to any hopes that the putrid odour sprang from my imagination.

"RUN!" I cried.

When you're alone outside at night, shrouded in total darkness, and someone yells that word, you take it at face value.

Howard's no exception.

He passed me as we bolted to the end of the road like race horses.

I felt something behind us. Something that made the ground shake. I could feel it even as I ran. Had my terrible dream become a reality? Could it really be that thing?

My bones wanted to jump out of my skin and

61

run on their own. I knew that by seeing one ghost already that night, it left the door wide open for other fantastic things to happen. It proved that the things I feared, but never thought were real, could touch and speak to me. Accepting that, I couldn't assume that whatever chased Howard and I onto Sawyer's bridge that night was anything less than the vile, dripping man-beast from that awful dream. The first of the four terrors.

When Howard tripped, I actually wanted to keep running . . . at first. But I stopped, grabbed him, and felt the breath of the monster blow over my neck. Its smell tried to crawl into my lungs, but I gritted my teeth and pulled Howard with me; way too hard.

We both fell to the ground.

I tried hard, very hard, not to look at it. It would only confirm my fears. It'd only make me scream.

I saw its silhouette.

A towering, shapeless mass, carrying itself like a giant child, brought itself forth from the darkness.

My eyes met the black, hollow sockets of the thing. Paralyzed by fear and fascination, I noticed that it did indeed have eyes; two moist, yellow balls set far back into its head. They locked onto us, and the beast's mouth opened, letting a glob of saliva spill down its beard.

Howard had been screaming the whole time.

I didn't, not until I saw the monster hoisting its club into the air, ready to make smeared human jam out of us to spread on who knows what.

"NO! OUT OF THE WAY!" I cried, digging my nails into Howard's arm and jerking him up. The beast brought its weapon smashing against the ground, shaking the entire bridge.

Howard got to his feet and we started to run, but the hulking giant stepped to cut us off.

The moonlight offered only hints of the monster's features, glistening tusks and the dripping snout. When it snarled, its row of teeth shone with spit, its tongue quivering for a taste of what trembled just a few feet away from it.

It brought the club in the air again.

"MITCH! OVER THE SIDE!" Howard yelled, and hopped the bridge's guard rail.

I went over with him, and as I cleared the rail, I saw him holding on for dear life on the other side. I held on, too, just as the monster's tree-sized club met the bridge road with thunderous results. The force of the blow almost shook us loose.

But we both held on. Our feet kicked below us into the open air. I heard water below, but couldn't see anything but a dark pool of black. Whimpers took the place of screams, and we waited for the monster's next move.

It leaned over the bridge.

It looked me straight in the eyes, I know it did.

Then it brought its club into the air one final time.

14

When the light hit the thing's face, I almost let go.

It seemed so impossible, so completely unreal that something would save us at the last second.

But it did.

One sharp beam of light struck the monster's head, sending it into a shrieking frenzy. The two moist, yellow eyeballs I mentioned before exploded. Its tongue rolled to the back of its mouth and I'm sure it choked on it before its head melted altogether, in veiny gobs of flesh that rained down on Howard and me.

We stopped our howling long enough to move out of the way as the behemoth tipped over the side, and dropped off into the blackness.

I never heard it hit bottom.

We heard someone crying in disbelief from the bridge road, then something dropped and footsteps slapped against the pavement.

Howard hoisted himself up first and gave me a hand. He slumped to the side of the rail and breathed heavy, secure breaths.

I stood, looking over the side to make sure the thing didn't return.

"Light. Light kills those things," I said.

Turning my attention to the bridge road, I saw a broken flashlight lying in pieces a few yards away. Walking closer, I recognized it instantly as the flashlight Ivan had used to search for us earlier.

He'd gotten more than he'd bargained for.

As I checked my pocket for the seal, and felt its cool, detailed indentations with my thumb, I couldn't help but think, *so did I.*

15

Howard and I didn't want to separate after that. After you see a monster and it tries to kill you, you just want to stick together. That's the best way I can describe what we felt.

When we reached his house, he didn't want to go in.

"I'm going to tell my Mom and Dad," he said. "We need help, and I don't care if we get in trouble."

"It won't matter if you tell them," I replied. "More monsters will come until I replace this seal. If everyone finds out we have the seal, the police will confiscate it, we'll go to prison, and they'll never let me near the museum. Maybe it's best if we figure this out ourselves."

"I don't know what to do," Howard admitted.

"I'll tell you what," I said. "I'll call you from

my house. We'll just gab for the rest of the night so I won't fall asleep. That way, no bad dreams. Is that cool with you?"

Howard grinned. "Yeah."

He went in, and I made my way back home. I called him the minute I got in and we did stay on the phone, talking about our experience, for most of the night. It wasn't until five o'clock in the morning that I finally fell asleep.

Plenty of time for a nightmare.

It ran like an instant replay in my head the entire next day at school.

Keri knew it too. I could see by her expression in class she'd been worrying, and when she dropped a note on my desk to meet her in the library after school, I knew she'd found something out.

Keri had volunteered to research the Deschaul exhibit. She knew Howard and I planned to return the seal on our own, but she wanted to know why the artefact held so much importance.

"I'll go ahead and tell you this," she whispered as I sat across from her in the practically deserted room of books. "You definitely should not have taken that seal."

"Tell me something I don't know," I replied, scanning the room for eavesdroppers.

She opened a spiral notebook full of notes and a few drawings. "I started by looking in this library, and came up with virtually nothing. Then I checked the article in the paper."

"Yeah, and . . . " I hated waiting for information.

"It gave the name of the museum in France where Mr. Deschaul acquired the exhibit. So then I e-mailed them, and pretty soon got into a chat session online with one of the cataloguers over there." Keri loved showing off her tech-know-how.

"What'd they say?" I asked.

"He gave me the name of the castle it originally came from. He said all the information they had on the exhibit came from the servants who worked there," she said.

"And did you get in touch with any of them?"

"He called one of them for me, but the guy pretty much gave the same story that was in the paper. The seal needs to be with the armour or a great curse will befall the land."

"So what did you do?"

"I got my friend to track down a servant of the castle who didn't work there any more. He gave me a name, and I did the rest. My parents' phone bill will never be the same."

"Was it worth it?" I asked.

"Let's just say that the former servants have an entirely different story when it comes to the seal and that green suit of armour."

16

Keri waited for the last few stragglers to walk out of the library door before she continued. Only the librarian, Mrs. Kendall, remained behind the desk, going through delinquent book slips, and eyeing the clock as the time approached closing.

"It happened sometime in the 1500s," Keri whispered.

"What happened?" I asked.

"Count Deschaul, monarch of a small province in France, mastered the art of sorcery, and sent his land plunging into an age of darkness," she explained.

"Count Deschaul was the man who wore the green armour." I'd figured out that much.

"Yep. But I also think I know who your ghost man is, and his story's not a happy one.

He was killed by Count Deschaul," she said, flipping over the notebook page to read the rest of her findings.

"Killed? How?"

"Well, the whole story is, the Count fell in love with a maiden in his land. I couldn't find her name, but she had already been spoken for by a knight, named Robáire, who served the Count. Robáire caught wind of the Count's infatuation, and decided to leave the province, taking the maiden with him." Keri had stopped reading from her notes. She'd memorized the story.

"So how did the Count kill Robáire?" I wanted to cut to the chase.

"Chill. I'm getting to that. Anyway, when you're a sorcerer, there aren't many things going on that you don't know about. He discovered Robáire's intentions, whereupon he kidnapped the maiden, and locked her in the castle's dark tower," Keri revealed. Her eyes got wider with every new twist of the tale.

"And then he killed Robáire?" I asked.

"No, not yet. He knew the good knight would fight valiantly to save his love, so he conjured up monsters to face Robáire at each of the three levels of the tower. The first of these creatures was a brutish ogre. It sounds like that's what attacked you and Howard. Then Deschaul created a vicious wild boar, larger than any that walked the earth. The final beast he called forth happened to be one of his oldest servants, a mythical griffin. It surpassed the other two in intelligence and viciousness, and the Count held him back as a last line of defence."

"I saw all of them in my dream," I told her. "Each of those things tried to kill me."

"I know," she said. "But you got through them. And so did Robáire. He reached the top of the dark tower to face Count Deschaul and save the maiden. It came down to a duel of swords."

"Who won?" I really had to know if Robáire's fate mirrored my own.

"Deschaul did. He was a sorcerer. Robáire never had a chance. The Count had been playing with him from the beginning. He put his sword through Robáire's chest, and the dying knight fell to his knees. But even as death was upon him, Robáire pleaded for the Count to release the maiden." Keri's eyes welled with tears. She didn't like this ending.

Neither did I. "So he let her go, right?" I asked.

Keri shook her head. "Deschaul told him he'd let her go if Robáire pledged him his own soul as payment. The good knight agreed and the Count produced a document right out of thin air, declaring Robáire's soul as his. Shaking and close to death, Robáire pulled his bloody, silver seal from under his armour, and stamped the document with his own crest. And so clinched the deal."

"And Robáire died?" I had to ask, my throat growing thick.

"And Robáire died. Deschaul never freed the maiden. Instead he forced her to live by his side until she died. He, himself, lived long after that, mastering the art of sorcery to the point that he no longer needed a land to live in. It's said he found ways to cross barriers of time and space, and that he left this world to explore new realms."

"This story really isn't very inspiring. What part does the seal play in all of this?" I asked.

"Well, the servant says this is how the story applies to the armour today. After Robáire's defeat, Deschaul wore the seal around his neck like a trophy. They say that when Robáire signed Deschaul's document, it transferred his soul not to the Count, but to the seal itself. So, as long as Deschaul wore the seal, he did indeed possess the remaining life of Robáire. But this would be his undoing."

"How?" I didn't understand. With Robáire dead, how could he threaten the Count?

"When Count Deschaul's magic grew to the point where he could leave this realm and experience new ones, Robáire's good soul acted just like a dimensional door lock," she explained.

"Huh?"

"When the Count last disappeared, he was wearing the armour that sits in the museum right now. Around that armour's neck, Deschaul wore the seal. Stories of his magic, and the curator himself faxed me a couple of them, say he returns in the same suit he leaves in. Actually they believe that's what ties him to all realms; a bunch of suits. Can you believe that? Anyway, the seal keeps him from re-entering this world inside the armour."

"But now that it's gone . . ."

"Now that it's gone, Deschaul is free to come home. And the seal you're trying to return. He doesn't want it back. It'd stop his homecoming," Keri said, eyeing Mrs. Kendall as she began to tidy things up to leave.

"But that's what I have to do," I said. "Otherwise . . ."

"Otherwise, a great darkness will befall our land," she said, just before Mrs. Kendall asked us to leave.

17

Suddenly, my nightmares made sense. The incredible encounter from the night before had a reason. The ogre wanted the seal.

All of the things that had happened to me since I took the artefact had a story behind them, and it took Keri only one night to find it.

"It's hard for me, you know, to act as if these things are real," she said as we walked to Howard's house after school. "You guys have seen them, but I've only heard your stories. I believe you, but it all sounds so impossible."

"Well, Howard and I were hanging off Sawyer bridge last night trying to get away from the impossible. It's real, all right," I said. The entire experience had a strange effect on me. After my first dream, where the images looked so vivid and felt so real, I could have almost actually believed it happened. It prepared me for the mental shock of seeing the ogre last night.

Poor Howard hadn't been given that sort of cushion. It really shook him up. I thought after we talked on the phone all night it would've calmed him down a bit, but no. When he didn't show up for school, I knew it would take more than a couple of talks to set Howard at ease again.

We cut through his neighbour's, the Taylor's, yard and came up behind his house. He sat in a rocking chair inside the glass sunroom. When he slowly waved us in, I noticed he wore a white housecoat, like you might see on a hospital patient. What was going on? The temperature in the room reminded me of the oven my great aunt lived in. She always kept it toasty, even in the summer. When we approached Howard, he looked wearily up at us, bags hanging from his eyes.

"Are you okay, Howard?" Keri asked.

"Okay? Heh, I'll never be okay," he said with a raspy, cynical voice. "I've seen something that just shouldn't be, and I'm not ever closing my eyes again."

"Howard, you're being very mela . . . melo . . ."

"Melodramatic," Keri helped out.

"Yeah, melodramatic. Listen, we've got a plan,

er, I mean an idea about how to get this seal back where it belongs, and Keri's going to help."

Howard looked at me, and then returned his gaze to the backyard. "An idea, you say. Uh, I don't want any part in it. Nope, no part."

"Howard, listen. We've already been to my house. The seal's in my pocket. Keri's going to the museum before it closes to unlock one of the windows. We'll climb in after everyone leaves and return the seal," I explained.

"I'm not going back. Don't you see, Mitch? Last night we saw a monster. To me, that's a sign. It says, 'Shape up, fly right, and don't sneak out of the house, Howard, or you'll see monsters'," my friend babbled.

"Howard," I said. "You dared me to take this seal, so we're in this together. And if we don't return it to where it came from, you're going to be seeing monsters all of the time."

Howard's face bunched in confusion, and Keri and I explained the whole story to him the best we could. It took a few minutes for him to accept the whole tale, but after considering our adventure on the bridge, he couldn't really argue. Soon Keri set off to the museum, giving her two hours before it closed. Howard and I waited out the time at his house.

I called over to tell Mom I'd be having dinner at Howard's. She sounded a little tense on the phone. She didn't really like Howard that much, believing him to be a bad influence on me. That brought out the guilty feelings I had for sneaking out without her knowing, and somewhere in the back of my mind, I knew I'd be paying for it sometime.

"Where are your parents, anyway?" I asked Howard as I hung up the phone.

"City Hall. Mr. Deschaul called a crime prevention meeting for tonight, and they went," he said, lacing up his sneakers. He ditched the housecoat for a sweatshirt and jeans.

I sighed heavily. "This has got to work tonight."

"I still don't see why we can't just leave it on the doorstep," Howard said.

"I told you. Robáire said I have to return it to its rightful place. Only I can do it. He's kind of placed me in charge of his soul or something," I explained, and then made my way to Howard's kitchen to raid the fridge. I yanked it open and found nothing but open space. "Hey, there's nothing to drink in here."

"Drink water," Howard yelled to the kitchen.

Grabbing a glass from the cabinet, I made my way over to the sink. That's when something passed in front of the kitchen window.

I only caught a glimpse of it, and thought, *the Peels are home. Meeting's over.*

But then I heard the tremendous squeal from outside, and something rammed into the wall.

The Wild Boar.

18

Howard ran into the kitchen just as the glasses and plates shot from the cabinets to crash on the floor.

"**WHAT IS IT?!**" he yelled, grabbing my shirt sleeve.

"**THE BOAR!**" I screamed, "**IT'S THE WILD BOAR!**"

We moved to the hallway, listening to the huffs and puffs of the huge beast as it dug in, circling outside the house at top speed.

"**WHERE'S IT GOING?!**" Howard yelled, running into the den. "**WHAT'S IT GOING TO DO?!**"

His answer came quickly, as the boar slammed into the side of the house, bursting through the panelling inside. Then it took off again.

"NO! NOT THE HOUSE!" Howard pleaded. Then we heard another wall being smashed in from the dining room.

"IT'S TRYING TO GET IN! WE'VE GOT TO GET SOMEWHERE SAFE!" I slapped him on the shoulder to snap him out of his shock. He followed me to the stairs just as the animal kicked through the front door!

"JUMP!"

"HELP ME!" Howard begged, as the beast wiggled its snarling head in further, dangerously close to the first stairs. I'd hopped over the banister already, and Howard desperately threw his arms into the air, screaming for me to pull him up. I reached down and grabbed his wrists, yanking him up as the boar pulled itself through the door.

It went directly for Howard's feet, but just missed them as my pal came crashing over the banister on top of me.

"GET OFF!" I screamed. The boar's head came smashing through the balustrade, and Howard couldn't get up! I pushed him off of me, and he started climbing the stairs as I slapped and kicked the monster's head to keep it away. With one foot, I got enough leverage to launch myself up a couple of steps, and then scrambled to get to my feet. The boar rounded the railing, and came up the stairs after us!

I heard a gurgling sob coming from Howard as we ran down the hall and into one of the bedrooms, where he slammed the door just after I slipped in.

"OUT THE WINDOW!" I yelled.

Howard held the door, looking confused. "Why? The . . ."

The door practically snapped in two pieces when the beast struck it. Howard jumped back to the wall, then bolted to the window and began pushing me through.

"JUST JUMP! HURRY!" Howard screamed, and then pushed me.

Twisting in the air, I dropped down on top of the metal that covered Howard's back porch, and landed right on my back. Howard came down right beside me.

"Is . . . is it coming after us?" I fought to ask.

"I . . . I don't know," Howard gasped.

Then, from the room where we jumped, the wall burst open, and out came the squealing monster.

We both moved to get out of its way as the

falling behemoth crashed through the centre of the covering.

I steadied myself against the edge of the covering's framework, waiting for it to collapse at any second with Howard and I on top. But it didn't.

Even with the huge hole in its centre, the porch shelter stayed standing. Howard had his back to me, bracing himself against the other side's edge, trembling. I inched my way to the hole, expecting to see a dead boar when I peeked over the edge.

But I didn't see anything.

19

"Howard," I whispered. "Howard. Do you see it over there?"

Howard whimpered.

"Howard, do you see it?" I asked again.

After a second, he shook his head, 'no'.

"Howard, listen. In my dream, I beat this thing. The boar killed itself by running through a glass showcase. It saw its own reflection, and thought it was another boar. It charged."

Howard turned his head to me. "So you don't think it's dead?" he asked.

"I don't think so," I replied, looking over the yard for the animal. "The ogre from last night died the same way it did in my nightmare. I just think that maybe these things happen in the same pattern."

"So what do you want to do?" Howard asked,

then peeked over his shoulder. "I don't feel safe up here. We're sitting ducks."

"Then let's run," I suggested.

"Where? Back inside? Down the street?" Howard was depending on me to make a decision.

"Since we don't see him, I think he either ran to the other side of the house, or he's inside. I don't know about you, but I'd rather take my chances outside," I told him, and he let things rattle around in his brain for a second.

"Okay, let's run," he said.

"Okay."

Lowering my head over the edge of the covering felt like I was offering the boar its supper. I just knew that at any second its teeth would clamp around my neck and that would be that. But to my relief, I still didn't see it.

"When my feet hit the ground, I'm running," I warned Howard.

"All right," he whispered.

I slid off the top of the covering, hung for a second, and then dropped to the porch. I hit the ground running.

"MITCH! THERE IT IS! BEHIND YOU!" Howard screamed.

From out of nowhere, the beast reappeared, and its mass moved like a locomotive straight for me.

My legs never stopped moving. I rounded the corner of the house, with no idea where to go next.

No cars coming by.

No neighbours in the street.

No one to run to for help.

I heard the boar puffing behind me, with short squeaks coming out of it every few steps. Rounding the second corner of Howard's house, I almost panicked. Then I remember thinking . . .

Glass . . .

just as I passed the sunroom near the end of my revolution around the house.

I heard Howard screaming at me from the covering as I shot through the backyard, arching my path just enough to loop back, and run directly for the sunroom.

The galloping beast moved with me, continuing its chase to the end.

I had no idea if it would work.

I'd put my trust in a nightmare.

For all I knew, that monster would run over me.

I cut through the grass, gritting my teeth,

and focusing on the glass until I got within five feet of it.

And then I slid onto the ground, like a baseball runner stealing home plate, and I stayed down.

Above me, glass shattered.

It came down on me, just like in the nightmare. But I closed my eyes, and it seemed like forever until the noise stopped.

When it did, everything fell deathly silent.

"Howard?" I asked.

"It's dead," he yelled down.

I opened my eyes and got up slowly so I wouldn't cut myself on any of the glass. On the other side of the shattered sunroom wall lay the wild boar, not bleeding, but not moving either.

"Are you sure it's dead?" I asked.

"Go kick it and make sure," Howard said.

No way.

Then suddenly, smoke began to billow from the creature's pores. In seconds, as Howard and I watched, the entire animal turned into yellow smoke and simply blew away. When the fog finally cleared, I saw the clock on the far wall.

"The museum," I said. "It's closed now. Let's get there before the next thing comes after us."

Howard stood looking at the devastation that he once called "home".

"Maybe I should leave a note," he said.

I grabbed him by the shirt and pulled him away from the mess. If we didn't succeed, the entire town might look the same way.

20

A cool wind blew leaves around us as we reached the museum. The building almost felt like an old acquaintance now, but not a very good one. I could almost see a sinister grin appear across its doorway. The columns looked like teeth. It waited for me, I knew it.

The crowds were gone. I checked my watch. Just a little after six. Everyone had packed up and gone home.

I scanned the grounds for security.

"No Ivan," Howard said as he came up behind me. He'd been wary of everything on the way over. He even jumped away from a few cats that crossed our path.

"There's no telling what seeing that ogre did to him," I said. "It might have scared him bad enough to leave town."

"Where's the window?" Howard asked.

"In the back. Come on," I said.

We walked along the edge of the trees, circling the museum just like the night before. I kept looking for signs of life, but nothing stirred. *Ivan must be somewhere around,* I kept thinking. *Things just aren't naturally this still.* Even the leaves had stopped falling. Every few steps, Howard would stop and look around like a deer being hunted. I just tightened my grip around the metal seal in my pocket. As soon as I saw that armour, I'd jam this seal in the helmet if I had to, and then take off, never to return to this menacing house of memories again.

"There it is," I said, pointing to a window just off the back left corner of the building.

"It's a little high. And there's nothing to climb onto," he said in a 'chickening out' tone.

"I'll stand on your shoulders and climb in," I said.

He looked relieved. How could anyone call me a coward if they haven't taken a good, close look at Howard Peel? He'd practically had the word tattooed on his head ever since the ogre incident. Still, if I wanted to pull this off, I'd have to depend on him.

We left the bushes, making our way across the

grass like a couple of Navy Seals. As soon as we got close to the wall, we threw ourselves against it, expecting to be surrounded by the enemy.

"So far so good," I whispered, then motioned with my hand for Howard to get into position.

He squatted in a catcher's stance, and braced his rear end against the wall. I stepped up on his shoulders and he lifted with his legs, grunting with his mouth closed. I grabbed the window handle. If Keri accomplished her mission, we'd be able to get in.

Locked.

I tugged harder. It couldn't be. No one ever came around to this corner of the museum. It's where they kept the mops and brooms and disinfectants.

Yep. Locked.

"Why won't it open?" Howard looked up and asked.

"It's locked. She promised it would be open. Something must have happened," I rationalized.

Howard bent over, signalling me to hop off.

"Maybe she just went home, and didn't come to the museum at all," he said.

"Keri? No way. She's as good as her word, you know that. Something had to have happened.

The museum might have closed early, or worse, they caught her at the window," I said, running all sorts of possibilities through my mind.

"Well, we're not getting in. Let's just go! I've got to get back to my house! My parents probably think I'm dead!" He pleaded so much that I gave in, against my better judgement. I didn't want to spend another night with the seal in my possession. But with no way in, and our parents most likely scouring town for us, it would probably be best if we went back home and confessed the whole thing. As long as I could talk my parents, the police, and Mr. Deschaul into letting me return the seal myself, I could live with any kind of punishment. Anything's better than getting attacked by monsters every night.

"Okay, let's go home," I said.

We rounded the corner of the museum, cutting through the front grass on our way to the street. At closer range this time, I took another look at the old building, and noticed something I hadn't seen before.

The door was open slightly. Even stranger, the video camera that had been above the door was now missing.

"Howard," I whispered. "Look."

He groaned as I walked to the front entrance, but came up behind me as I crept to the door, and slid in.

21

"*Mitchell Garrison,*" said a familiar voice. "*Come in.*"

My heart hung in my chest like a wet sack.

I heard Howard turn and go for the door, and when I whipped around to follow, I saw it slam shut just as Howard got to it.

"*And you, too, Howard,*" the voice finished.

The griffin, here in the museum.

But where? I couldn't see it. I could only hear its voice.

We moved to the centre of the foyer, watching every corner of the room for something to jump out at us.

"*You have come to do battle with Count Deschaul,*" said the griffin. "*You must first pass this gate.*"

Just like in the dream. I knew what would be coming next . . .

"*To pass this gate, you must guess my name. You have*

three guesses," it said.

Howard froze in his spot. "Th . . . Then I'm not saying a word," he quivered. "I don't want to pass this gate."

"You must guess, or I chew off your head. If all of your guesses are wrong, I leave your heads on, so you can see everything I do to you. In the end you'll not only wish you guessed right, but that I'd chewed off your heads to begin with," the griffin vilely announced. It hadn't seemed as brutal in my nightmare.

Howard started whimpering and circling the floor, looking for some way out. When he got near the doorway leading to the first exhibits, I heard the flapping of alerted wings echoing through the entire museum.

"HOWARD, STOP! STAY WHERE YOU ARE!" I yelled.

Even through his panic, he listened to me. I slowly made my way over to him and grabbed his shirt, pulling him back with me to the centre of the foyer.

"There is a time limit," it called to us.

My friend shook uncontrollably, and I held his arm tightly to make sure he didn't fall apart.

"You . . . you had the nightmare. What is this thing?" Howard stammered.

"It's called a griffin," I told him.

"GRIFFIN!" Howard called. "YOU'RE A GRIFFIN!"

"HOWARD, NO!" I yelled.

"My name is not A Griffin," it answered.

"GRIFFIN, THEN! JUST GRIFFIN!" Howard continued shouting.

"HOWARD, I'M GOING TO KILL YOU!" I swore, then threw my friend down to the ground, my hand over his mouth and my fist in the air.

Howard's eyes watered up in fear and I could feel him trembling under my tightening grip.

What was I doing?

Acting just like Kyle Banner, *the bully I hate*.

I took my hand off of Howard's mouth and sat on the floor with my face in my hands.

"My name is not A Griffin and my name is not Griffin. You have one more guess," the griffin said to us.

My mind tried to focus on what saved me in the dream. *The design. Like a child's puzzle game. What did it look like?*

That's it. That's what it looked like! I could see every shape in my head! Quickly, I ran over to the museum's front desk and grabbed a paper and pencil. It's like something possessed my hand. In just seconds, I'd drawn the design exactly as it appeared in my dream!

My eyes ran over it again and again. What could it mean?

"*Come now, boy. The time. The time . . .*" warned the griffin.

Think, Mitchell, think! I told myself. *Black shapes, white shapes . . . What are they saying to me?*

WAIT.

Maybe . . .

With the pencil I drew a line into the puzzle.

An 'R'! That's it! I kept going!

Within seconds, I had the puzzle solved.

"Rothmore. *Your name is Rothmore,*" I said.
There was no reply.

I felt a cold, spreading doom coating my
skin, waiting on something to make a noise.
Anything.

*Suddenly the beast dropped from out of the
shadows, landing in a spot of natural moonlight
just to the right of me. It came forward in long,
stalking steps, backing me up until I felt my feet
trip together!*

*I fell on my back and within a blink the crea-
ture was upon me, breathing over my face,
READY TO CHEW MY HEAD . . .*

"*Thank you,*" said the griffin.

"Thank you?!" I repeated, totally confused. *"ROTHMORE?"*

"That is my name," said Rothmore. *"A curse was put upon me by Count Deschaul. I would remain in his servitude until a mortal guessed my real name. You have done that, and now I am free."* Rothmore then turned around and headed for the door. He stopped at the doorway, and turned around to say, *"Thank you, once again."*

"Wait!" I called to him. "Can you help me? I need to return this seal!" I tore it from my pocket and held it in the air for the griffin to see.

"The Count awaits you through those doors. Good luck," Rothmore said, and then crept out the door, letting it slam shut behind him.

Howard had fainted. I stepped over him to check the entrance door. I couldn't budge it.

Then someone screamed, **"MITCHELL!"**

I knew who it was. *Keri.*

22

I spun the seal's leather strap tightly around my hand, making the artefact look like nothing more than a highly detailed joybuzzer. I figured if I kept it close, I'd stay safe.

I couldn't be sure the scream came from Keri. After all, if Count Deschaul had really come back to life, he was a sorcerer supreme. He could make any noise he wanted.

I stepped into the darkness of the first main exhibit hall, frantically searching the wall for a light switch, but I couldn't find one. So I made my way through the dark.

Every shape in the room threatened me. I expected the exhibits to step out after me at any second; the town's first stagecoach rolling to life, or the mannequins of the town's first football team, the Green Devils, jumping down from their show stands and attacking me. I could see the outlined head of the Praying Mantis, on tour with the Bug Around animatronic bug show, lowering its head and taking a bite out of me with its pincers.

Blue lights flashed outside the oversized, arch windows. Four police cars drove by the museum, more than likely on their way to Howard's. I watched them as they passed, and in the strobing flashes of their lights, I noticed something in the corner of the room.

The armour.

Even in a dark room, filled with so many exhibits, it was hard to miss.

It stood against the wall, alone and unmoving.

Where's Keri? I wondered.

Maybe it had been a trick, but from whom? The armour looked empty.

Then I heard someone scream my name again.

From behind me.

Spinning around, I quickly zeroed in on its source; through the dark archway leading into the next exhibit hall.

I went lightly, expecting something to jump out of the dark and strike me at any moment. I watched every shadow for movement.

The scream came again.

Just as I approached the archway, I decided to run through. Whatever was waiting in that room wouldn't expect that.

I darted into the darkness, only to be welcomed by faint beams of moonlight through the windows, and something barely moving in the corner.

I couldn't tell what it was. I had to get closer.

Grand tapestries and assorted weapons hung from the walls, and pedestals with small exhibits encased in glass dotted the floor. Everything seemed so . . . familiar. I used each display to my advantage, moving from one to another as if they were trees in the woods. I finally got to the exhibit, not ten feet from where the moving shadow sat.

"Mitchell . . . is that you?" it asked.

Keri.

Above her head, that sign . . .

THE DESCHAUL MEDIEVAL EXHIBIT

If this is the medieval exhibit, what's the knight doing out there . . ?

"MITCHELL, BEHIND YOU!"

Instinctively, I ducked and rolled forward.

From the ground, I saw the EMERALD KNIGHT swinging his sword through the space of air where my head had just been.

Its echoing laughter filled the hall, followed by the red glow that spilled through the armour's visor from whatever furnace fuelled it from inside.

COUNT DESCHAUL

HAD RETURNED . . .

23

Grabbing Keri's hand and nearly yanking it off, I pulled her up and along with me across the floor.

The armour continued its cackling, swinging its sword at us again. It came nowhere near hitting us, and it seemed almost like a taunting gesture, telling us the games had just begun.

We bolted through the archway, back out into the darkness of the first exhibit hall. It didn't take me long to plow right into one of the displays, sending it, along with Keri and myself rolling to the floor.

Stupid mannequin, I thought, as I looked down at it. *This isn't a mannequin, it's . . . it's . . .*

The armour entered the room, and its illuminated visor revealed the face of what I'd crashed into.

"MR. DESCHAUL!" I screamed.

It was him, but he'd been changed. The evil Count had turned his modern-day descendant into *stone*. Pure stone, smooth yet solid to the touch. A look of ultimate horror had been left on his face, and his hands were outstretched with clawing fingers.

Keri screamed as the knight appeared over us. This time I didn't have to grab her. She led the way. We ran back into the foyer, where I saw Howard coming to, looking at us like he just got out of bed.

I instinctively tried the door again.

"IT'S STILL LOCKED! HOWARD! GET UP!" I yelled.

"WHY?" he asked, and then I can only assume he saw the oncoming red light overtaking the main exhibit hall and making its way to the foyer. He jumped to his feet, and I felt him pushing my back as we followed Keri up a short flight of stairs.

Most of the rooms up there were offices. Tiny orange and green lights from computers and fax machines served as guides down the hall. When we couldn't see them any more, we stopped. So did the hall. We found ourselves standing on a balcony overlooking the medieval exhibit.

Completely trapped.

I ducked back to the side of the doorway along with Howard and Keri.

"What are we going to do?" Keri quietly asked.

"Let's jump for it," whispered Howard.

"We'll break our legs jumping from this high. Then we'd really be sitting ducks!"

"Why don't you throw the seal at him?" Howard snapped.

"I can't just throw the seal at him! It has to stay on him somehow!" I shot back.

"We've got to figure something out! I don't want to end up like Mr. Deschaul!" Keri said, before she heard the sound.

Crashing, metal footsteps.

Coming up the stairs.

I wondered how the thing had ever managed to sneak up on me with footsteps like that. It moved slowly, the stomping growing louder.

I could see everyone taking deep breaths, ready to run even if we didn't know where. My heart practically dented my chest as it slammed into it again and again.

The steps became less muffled, echoing through the hallway. Then, suddenly . . .

they stopped.

"**Mitchell Garrison**," called the vein-pinching voice. "**Please come out.**"

It used the same icy tone as in my dream; that same chilling, commanding voice that ordered me to obey.

But I didn't. I stayed behind the corner, hugging the wall like I could squeeze an escape plan from it.

"**What are the consequences for the things you have done?**" it slyly asked.

The results of my crime began rolling through my head. Bad nightmares, the destruction of Howard's house, poor Mr. Deschaul, and . . .

"**Very often**," he said, "**others pay for your actions! Your friends with you now will most definitely pay.**"

No! Keri had nothing to do with it! Howard talked me into it, but he's paid his price! I couldn't let my friends suffer for a crime I'd committed!

I rose, and turned the corner.

There, at the end of the hall, stood the motionless suit of armour. The fire in its eyes had died out, and its arm no longer held an upraised sword.

"They have nothing to do with this," I said. "You want me." It took every bit of courage I had to keep my voice together, and my body from shaking apart.

I waited for a response. For a few seconds, it didn't move or say a word. I started getting excited, thinking that maybe I'd just been seeing things. Maybe the armour never moved at all. Maybe someone had just set it at the top of the stairs.

"**I WANT THE SEAL DESTROYED!**" it screamed. Light burst from its head, and cut into my eyes, almost blinding me. I tried to back up, but my legs wouldn't work. Falling to the floor, I saw the horrifying outline of the metal suit as it marched toward me.

"**My three creatures failed me. You defeated them all. But history will repeat itself, and the hero will die by my hand!**" he threatened, raising his sword above his head.

The end of my nightmare was about to come true.

Then someone grabbed the armour from behind.

"GET BACK, KID! I'VE GOT THIS THING!"

24

IVAN!

He wrestled with the Count, climbing on the armour's back as it rammed him into the wall time after time. Ivan fell off and the knight grabbed him by the throat, dragged him down the hall, then lifted him and slammed him up against the end wall.

My vision cleared, and I felt someone yanking my collar.

"LET'S GET OUT OF HERE!" Howard screamed in my ear.

"We can't get by them," I told him, watching Ivan's face bunch up under the strain.

Then, with an inhuman effort, Ivan wrapped his legs around the armour, and used the leverage to pull both of them from the wall . . . and down the stairs.

111

The sounds of them smashing against walls and stairs scared us to the core. We didn't want to move.

Then Ivan screamed, a long, terror-stricken wail that curdled my blood and sent Keri's nails digging into my arm.

Then it stopped.

Total silence.

None of us knew what to do. I took Keri's hand and loosened her death-grip from my forearm. Howard helped me to my feet, quickly positioning himself behind me. He and Keri wanted to know if everything was safe, and so did I. But no one wanted to take that peek by themselves.

I took the first step. My feet felt as if they'd been rooted to the floor. The sweat that had beaded on my forehead disappeared as I reached the stairs, and fear chilled me to the bone.

"Ivan . . ?" I called.

No answer.

"Ivan . . ?"

THE KNIGHT STEPPED FROM THE DARKNESS. Count Deschaul had defeated Ivan, and now he wanted us.

Keri and Howard screamed in terror, running back to the balcony. Howard had tried to pull me with them, but I held my ground and pulled out the seal.

The Count stopped at first, but instantly recovered and continued his advance.

"IVAN! IVAN!" I called.

"**Ivan is now the stone twin of that relative of mine, Mr. Deschaul. Do not worry, it wears off. But what I am going to do to you will not!**"

With Count Deschaul stalking me from the front, and Keri and Howard crying behind me, focusing couldn't have been any more difficult.

"**Throw up the seal, boy, so I can melt it in the air!**" He dropped his sword, and the hand that held it began to glow green.

That's when I decided to risk the broken legs.

I spun around, ran to the balcony and prepared to jump to the floor below!

"MITCHELL, NO!" Keri screamed.

"**HOLD STILL, MITCHELL!**" I heard the Count command.

I turned to see his glowing hand produce a green ball of fire that he quickly lobbed my way.

I ducked. The ball shot over me and exploded into a shower of sparks on the far wall.

As I rose, my eyes caught sight of the huge

tapestry hanging on the wall. Without listening to any of the warnings outside or inside my head, I jumped for it, *and caught hold!*

I twisted my body enough to see Count Deschaul emerge from the hallway, *ready to launch another fireball my way!*

Howard and Keri attacked him, tackling his legs and arms, trying to bring him down. But he held fast, and when he raised his arm to cast the flame at me, I felt the tapestry give. One side of it came off the wall and swung me outward.

I held on for dear life with my right hand, and clutched the seal's strap tightly with my left.

The Count took his shot, and it looked like it was just going to miss me. Then I realized he wasn't aiming at me . . . *He was aiming at the seal in my hand!*

The fireball struck the seal! I instantly felt it fly from my grasp, but couldn't hear it hit the floor.

Then the whole tapestry gave a little.

I started climbing down as fast as I could, but . . . *the whole thing gave way before I could make it all the way to the ground.*

25

Everything hit the floor at once. Along with the tapestry and myself, all of the other exhibits that had been mounted on the wall came crashing to the floor in one giant medieval heap.

I crawled out of the mess to see Count Deschaul floating off the ground with Howard hanging onto his legs! The balcony floor was just underneath Howard's dangling feet.

I'd completely run out of options when I saw a puddle of liquid glowing brightly on the ground. *The seal.* The blast had melted it! But just a couple of feet away from it lay an object that gave me a desperate idea.

The crossbow.

Howard's words rang in my head.

He laid out Arsenal, the one-man weapon, with a crossbow. It was the only thing that would pierce the bad guy's armour.

I grabbed the crossbow just as I heard Howard scream and fall back down to the balcony. I could expect the Count to follow at any second.

Counting my blessings that the fall hadn't inadvertently launched the crossbow's arrow, I picked up the weapon and lowered the tip of the arrow into the melted seal, coating the entire arrowhead.

I finished just as the Emerald Sorcerer lowered himself to the floor.

"Now, let us do this face to face," he said, and took off his helmet, revealing a head that blazed the same bright green as his hand. Two eyes and a mouth could barely be made out, but I could tell that Count Deschaul's body would soon be whole again.

"I cannot fully cross over until that cursed seal has been completely dissolved! You are going to help me, Mitchell! I am going to pour its melted form into this helmet, and make you swallow every last drop. Then I am going to make your friends my slaves, and this town will serve as my new kingdom! You will be known to the people of this town as the boy who doomed them all! Your name will be synonymous with loss and despair!"

I held the crossbow up and aimed it, but I could hardly keep it steady . . .

"Anything's better than Moonwalker," I said, and launched the arrow.

It pierced Count Deschaul's breastplate, bringing him to a halt. Even through the glaring light that was his head, I saw his surprise. His hands grabbed the arrow and pulled on it, trying to yank it free, but his power began to fade. The glow he emitted started to dim, and then seemed to short-circuit like a television going on the blink. The arrow had stopped him, and the soul of the noble Robáire would at last have its revenge!

"NNOOOOOOOOOOOOO! IT CANNOT END LIKE THIS! NOT LIKE THIS!" he screamed out. The green flashes came faster, and the Count's head faded, leaving a droning, agonizing moan behind.

Another green flash.

Then another.

And the plug had been pulled. The Count's armour dropped to the ground, empty.

I fell back on the tapestry, finally letting all the air I had sucked in escape my lungs, and I placed the crossbow over my heart.

I saw the ghostly image of Robáire appearing on the balcony just as Keri and Howard ran out. He looked happy.

"**Thank you**," he said simply.

26

Howard ran into the exhibit hall, and kicked the Count's helmet all the way across the room. Keri darted straight to me, and shook me to make sure I was still alive.

"I'm okay! I'm okay!" I yelled.

"Is he really gone? He can't come back, can he?" she asked.

"After all the screaming he did? No, he's gone, all right," I told her.

"What about Ivan? He's been turned completely to stone, just like Mr. Deschaul." She wanted too many answers, too soon.

"I don't know. The Count said it wouldn't last long. We'll just have to take his word for it!" I explained, hoping he had been telling the truth.

"The door's still locked," Howard said. "I tried it when we came down. I guess we'll have to use a window to get out!"

"I'm not leaving. I'm waiting for someone to find us here," I told him.

"WHAT?! ARE YOU CRAZY?! The place is wrecked! If we leave now, no one will ever know we had anything to do with this. The seal's even melted away! There's no evidence! Let's get out of here!" he raved.

"No way. I never should've taken that seal to begin with, but if I don't confess to doing it, I would be getting away with something worse. All of the after-effects, the consequences, would've happened for no reason at all. I've got to stay, but if you want to leave, go ahead."

Howard frowned and sulked around for a few moments, but then said, "Okay. I'll stay. It's outrageously stupid, though."

"It's brave," Keri said thoughtfully. "But listen, we'd better go check on Mr. Deschaul and Ivan."

I got up slowly, and we walked through the arches to the main exhibit hall. I turned and took one last glance back at the empty pile of armour laying on the floor.

I'd done it. I'd defeated Count Deschaul and lifted the curse from the noble Robáire's tortured soul. I'd never felt better about myself.

Even in the darkness of the main hall, I felt safe. Nothing scared me, not even telling the truth about the seal. Confessing my crime to Mr. Deschaul would be hard, but it had to be done.

"Howard, find the light," I said. "I can't see a thing in here."

"No problem," he said, walking over to the wall and feeling along for a switch.

After this, I told myself, *I'll always face my problems head on. I'll be brave. No more backing up or running away.*

Howard finally found the lights, flipped them on, and instantly a scream erupted from Keri's lungs.

There, on the floor, lay Mr. Deschaul's stone body.

Broken in half.

I almost fell over, but Keri grabbed me, and sobbed, *"When you ran into him, he must have hit the floor and broken!"*

"COME ON, MITCH!" yelled Howard. **"NO ONE SAW IT HAPPEN! LET'S GET OUT OF HERE!"**

"Mitchell! We can't leave him this way! We can't! We have to try to help him!" Keri pleaded.

"MITCH! THERE'S NO HELPING THAT GUY! LET'S RUN!"

It seemed I had a decision to make, and now I had the courage to make the *right* one.

But all things considered, *I wished it had all been just a nightmare.*

27

Of course, we never told Mr. Deschaul about breaking him in half.

He didn't remember a thing. He didn't recall being attacked by the knight, and had no idea the evil suit of armour turned him to stone.

So we didn't feel any need to worry him further by telling him we used some quick drying cement that the renovation workers had left to put him back together. When he returned to normal, he never felt a thing.

Ivan, however, seems to remember everything, though he hasn't said anything to let anyone know for sure. My bet's that this encounter has fuelled him to step up his personal mission to secure Fairfield from outside dangers. He even investigated the mysterious trashing of Howard's house to get a good idea about what measures he'll have to take to ensure the town's safety.

And me, well, I confessed to Mr. Deschaul that I took the seal. I didn't implicate Howard, but he bucked up and admitted his involvement, too. Mr. Deschaul didn't press any charges, but Howard and I will have our weekends planned for us for quite some time. It turns out there's plenty of work to do around the museum for two boys being punished.

As far as my 'Moonwalker' nickname goes, it's changed to 'Sticky Fingers'. It seems my little stunt didn't impress anyone after all.

And since my confrontation with Count Deschaul, I feel more than confident I can handle Kyle Banner now. The problem is, he's the only one who thinks what I did is cool.

So, anyway, my reputation has changed, even if it's not really for the better.

But that's not what bothers me.

You see, since the adventure, my nightmares have stopped. In fact, I haven't had any dreams at all.

It's given me a very uncomfortable feeling.

Like something sinister's on the horizon.

If a suit of armour can come to life and cre-

ate monsters like an ogre and a wild boar, what other supernatural horrors could be out there? Rothmore, the griffin, for one. *But what about others?*

Those cold feelings, sensations of dread and oncoming doom, test my new-found courage when ill winds blow in the dark of night.

I miss my bad dreams.

At least they warned me about the terrifying things to come.

My advice, listen to your nightmares. *They just might be right!*

And now an exciting preview of the next

™

11
Something Rotten
by Marty M. Engle

1

"Hey, Joe! You just about finished? I want to go home!" my little brother whined, walking in a circle, staring at his size six sneakers as they kicked up a dry cloud of dust. Gary didn't like this field. It was too big. Too barren. Too dusty. Warm spring days like today made the cracked, dry ground seem anxious for a cooling shower.

Gary spit, as if to comply with the ground's wishes, and kicked over a rock, the very goal of our expedition. Behind him, our suburban neighbourhood stretched out in full view, spreading across the valley below.

"Got one!" I yelled excitedly, pulling the rock from the ground. "Feldspar Granite." At least that's what it looked like. Like most igneous rocks, granite is pretty easy to find. I turned the pinkish, speckled chunk over in my gloved hand as I raised it up, holding it against the bright blue sky. "A good one, too."

"Hoorah. Hurray. Let's go," Gary mumbled sarcastically, not even looking up.

"Could you at least fake interest for a moment?" I yelled, fumbling through the green canvas sack slung across my shoulder.

I slid it off and put it down on the ground in front of me, so I could find a specimen container more easily. "Do you even know what Feldspar Granite is?"

"It's what your head's made of," Gary sighed, bending over and picking up a pebble.

"You're a riot, Gary. You need your own show on Fox or something. You, Hank and Darren could be the stars. Call it 'Bratty Little Brothers' or something. 'A bold, fresh look at dorky siblings and the people they annoy'."

"It'd come on right after 'Skinny Joe Alister's World of the Weak'," Gary laughed, cracking himself up.

"DON'T CALL ME THAT! You know I HATE that!" It's true. I'm skinny. *Way* skinny.

Shrimpy even. Gary's the same way though, so he doesn't have a lot of room to talk. Our white t-shirts hang on us like sacks.

I growled, popping the lid off a rock container I fished from the canvas bag. It looked like a plastic jar that pills would come in. I plunked the chunk of rock inside and carefully wrote the date on the label.

I went rock collecting in the field after school, hoping it would cheer me up. Gary tagged along as usual, as if under contract.

We were both in lousy moods. I had been publicly humiliated at school that day, and Gary . . . well, Gary's always in a bad mood, unless he's in front of the TV.

"You know, I can't believe Shelly Miller actually *bench-pressed* you," Gary said.

"AWW, MAN! You think I wanna talk about that?" The bitter source of today's humiliation.

"Sorry, but straight up? Five times? Not even a strain, just . . ." Gary made a motion like a weight-lifter, pushing up a barbell from his chest.

"ALL RIGHT! ALL RIGHT, already! Enough! I don't want to talk about it," I cried.

David Donaldson and Shelly Miller got into a big fight about who was stronger and made a bet: who could bench-press *me* the most times. Actually the *Joe Alister, living-barbell* part was Darren Donaldson's idea. Darren's flair for striking visuals and his friendship with Gary led to my involvement.

Absurd? Yes. Humilating? Yes. But Shelly Miller sure is stronger than she looks.

Oh, they were nice about it, of course. They asked if I would do it, and like an idiot, *I agreed.* What could I do? Everyone was saying, "Please? C'mon. Be a pal. Be a sport. It's all in good fun, blah, blah, blah . . ."

How embarrassing. Still, I'm kind of used to it. Being the smallest kid at Fairfield Junior High is tough. Everyone looks down on me. Even Kyle Banner usually deems me unworthy of his barbaric attention.

"We've been out here for three hours. Can we go home now, please? There's this device in our living room called television that I need to sit in front of as much as possible." Gary's arm snapped up over his head and he flung something . . .

A small rock hit the ground right beside me and bounced up into my shin.

"HEY! Watch it! You could have hit me in the . . . hey, wait a minute. What was it you threw?" Gary wouldn't know a rare rock if he was holding it, *or* throwing it.

He watched me scour the ground and rolled his eyes in disbelief. "Oh man, give me a break! Excuse me, Sherlock, but it was just a stupid pebble! A nothing! A nobody among rocks. Just one of the ordinary, faceless sedimentary crowd."

I found it, popped it in a plastic jar and placed my new prize into the bag, another beauty to add to my growing collection. "These are igneous, not sedimentary, and there is no such thing as an ordinary rock. Every rock is different."

"Okay. I give up. I'm going back without you."

"Fine," I mumbled, bending over to check out a shiny, black pebble.

"I mean it!" Gary yelled.

"Great. Go. Bye."

He stopped. "Aw c'mon, Joe. 'Creature Features' will be on soon. You want to see it, too. I know you do."

If they gave trophies for tantrum-throwing, nasally whines, or over-dramatic sympathy ploys, Gary wouldn't have an empty shelf. But this time, he was right. I wanted to see the show, too.

"All right. Let's go."

I took one last, long look out across Fairfield, a thousand dots of light in a darkening valley. It sure looked nice from up here.

The sun began to set.

"C'mon, Joe. It's a good one tonight, it's 'The Blob!'"

READ MORE IN PENGUIN

In every corner of the world, on every subject under the sun, Penguin represents quality and variety – the very best in publishing today.

For complete information about books available from Penguin – including Puffins, Penguin Classics and Arkana – and how to order them, write to us at the appropriate address below. Please note that for copyright reasons the selection of books varies from country to country.

In the United Kingdom: Please write to *Dept. EP, Penguin Books Ltd, Bath Road, Harmondsworth, West Drayton, Middlesex UB7 ODA*

In the United States: Please write to *Consumer Sales, Penguin USA, P.O. Box 999, Dept. 17109, Bergenfield, New Jersey 07621-0120*. VISA and MasterCard holders call 1-800-253-6476 to order Penguin titles

In Canada: Please write to *Penguin Books Canada Ltd, 10 Alcorn Avenue, Suite 300, Toronto, Ontario M4V 3B2*

In Australia: Please write to *Penguin Books Australia Ltd, P.O. Box 257, Ringwood, Victoria 3134*

In New Zealand: Please write to *Penguin Books (NZ) Ltd, Private Bag 102902, North Shore Mail Centre, Auckland 10*

In India: Please write to *Penguin Books India Pvt Ltd, 706 Eros Apartments, 56 Nehru Place, New Delhi 110 019*

In the Netherlands: Please write to *Penguin Books Netherlands bv, Postbus 3507, NL-1001 AH Amsterdam*

In Germany: Please write to *Penguin Books Deutschland GmbH, Metzlerstrasse 26, 60594 Frankfurt am Main*

In Spain: Please write to *Penguin Books S. A., Bravo Murillo 19, 1° B, 28015 Madrid*

In Italy: Please write to *Penguin Italia s.r.l., Via Felice Casati 20, I–20124 Milano*

In France: Please write to *Penguin France S. A., 17 rue Lejeune, F–31000 Toulouse*

In Japan: Please write to *Penguin Books Japan, Ishikiribashi Building, 2–5–4, Suido, Bunkyo-ku, Tokyo 112*

In Greece: Please write to *Penguin Hellas Ltd, Dimocritou 3, GR–106 71 Athens*

In South Africa: Please write to *Longman Penguin Southern Africa (Pty) Ltd, Private Bag X08, Bertsham 2013*